This Boxer Books paperback belon

. . . . 'MBE AND C(. . . . .

www.boxerbooks.com

Splish-Splosh

Nicola Smee

Boxer Books

"Who wants a ride
in my little boat?"
asks Mr Horse.

"We do, please, Mr Horse," say Cat and Dog and Pig and Duck.

Mr Horse rows out to sea.
Splish, splash
go the oars.

"Can we have a go, please, Mr Horse?" ask Cat and Dog and Pig and Duck.

"That's a good idea," says Mr Horse. "My arms were getting very tired."

The waves get bigger...

splish, splash!

And bigger...
splish, splash!

And
bigger...!

And what do you think
happens next?

Cat and Dog and Pig
and Duck FALL OUT
of the little boat ...

Splish, splash, splosh!

Into the deep, blue sea!

But where, oh where
is Mr Horse?

"Help! Help! Help! Help!"
cry Cat
and Dog
and Pig
and Duck.

"Here I am!" says Mr Horse.

"Now hold on TIGHT!"

Splish, splash

go the waves ...

Splish, splash, splosh!

Back to the beach.

"AGAIN!"

cry Cat
and Dog
and Pig
and Duck.

"Come on, then,"
laughs Mr Horse.
And off they go again.

Splish, splash, splosh!

For SOPHIA, ZAKI and CHROME HOOF
Nicola Smee

First published in hardback in Great Britain in 2011 by Boxer Books Limited.
First published in paperback in Great Britain in 2012 by Boxer Books Limited.
www.boxerbooks.com

Text and illustrations copyright © 2011 Nicola Smee

The right of Nicola Smee to be identified as the author and
illustrator of this work has been asserted by her
in accordance with the Copyright, Designs and Patents Act, 1988.

The illustrations were prepared using an ink line and watercolour on handmade paper.
The text is set in Baskerville MT Schoolbook.

ISBN 978-1-907967-23-8

1 3 5 7 9 10 8 6 4 2

Printed in Singapore

All of our papers are sourced from managed forests and renewable resources.

More Boxer Books Paperbacks to enjoy

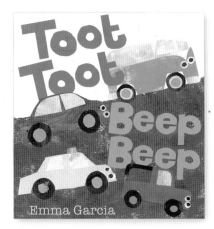

Toot Toot Beep Beep • _Emma Garcia_

Toot Toot Beep Beep is a fun, bright book for young children. Colourful cars zoom across the page, each making their own special noise. Little ones will love joining in with the sounds, making this book perfect for reading aloud. _Toot Toot Beep Beep_ is the follow-up to the highly successful _Tip Tip Dig Dig_, which was shortlisted for the Read It Again! Picture Book Award for an outstanding debut picture book.

ISBN 978-1-906250-51-5

Clip-Clop • _Nicola Smee_

Cat, Dog, Pig and Duck all want to climb aboard Mr Horse for a ride. But when they get bored with the slow pace, they ask Mr Horse to go faster and faster ... But will "faster" lead to disaster? A delightful rhythmical text with adorable illustrations which will enthral every child.

'... it just has to be enjoyed all over again, once the end is reached. And again ... and again!' Books for Keeps

ISBN 978-1-905417-04-9

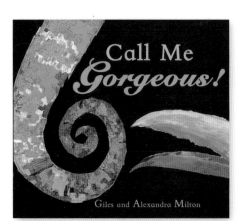

Call Me Gorgeous! • _Giles Milton & Alexandra Milton_

Discover a mysterious and fabulous creature in this beautiful book from Giles and Alexandra Milton. It has a porcupine's spines and a crocodile's teeth, a chameleon's tail and a cockerel's feet. What on earth could it be?

'A debut picture book that not only deserves to be examined closely, but also stood well back from and gazed at in awe.' Bookseller

ISBN 978-1-907152-49-8

The Art of Storytelling

www.boxerbooks.com